J acob found the owl in the nearby woods. Because of a broken wing, it could not take care of itself. Jacob sheltered the owl in the shed by his house, and fed it the game it could no longer catch for itself. He called his new friend Owl.

Owl made Jacob forget how hard it was to make friends with other boys and how different he found living in rural Maine instead of the city. Owl could even make him forget how much he missed his father, who no longer lived with Jacob and his mother but was thousands of miles away.

No one was going to come between Jacob and Owl—neither his mother nor the kindly director of the local bird sanctuary.

Sensitive and accurate, this is the moving story of a boy's love for an owl and the lessons about life he learns from his involvement. Striking photographs complement the text.

JACOB AND OWL

Jacob and Owl

A STORY

BY ADA AND FRANK GRAHAM

PHOTOGRAPHS BY FRANK AND DOROTHEA STOKE

COWARD, McCANN & GEOGHEGAN · NEW YORK

Library of Congress Cataloging in Publication Data

Graham, Ada.
  Jacob and owl.

  Summary: A lonely young boy nurses an owl back to health, then must make the difficult decision about the bird's future.
  [1. Owls—Fiction] I. Graham, Frank, 1925-   . II. Stoke, Frank. III. Stoke, Dorothea. IV. Title.
  PZ7.G75166Jac   [Fic]   81-3119
  ISBN 0-698-20516-2   AACR2

First printing

Designed by Lynn Braswell

Printed in the United States of America

For Chandler and Marion Richmond
of the Birdsacre Wildlife Sanctuary, Ellsworth, Maine

Contents

ABOUT THIS BOOK

Injured wild owls are often found in this country and are cared for by kind people. The owl that appears in the photographs in this book is named Ollie. He is a real owl. He had some of the adventures that we tell about in our book.

But this is a story. Most of the details have been made up, and the people who appear in the story are imaginary.

We would like to thank Chandler Richmond, Director of the Birdsacre Wildlife Sanctuary in Ellsworth, Maine, for his cooperation in permitting us to take photographs of the birds at the sanctuary.

We would also like to thank Joshua Bewig of Waterville, Maine, for his skill and patience in posing for the photographs of our leading character, Jacob.

ADA AND FRANK GRAHAM
FRANK AND DOROTHEA STOKE

A Mysterious Stranger

Jacob first heard about the owl on the bus that carried him home from school. Two other boys were talking softly in the seat behind him.

"When we get home let's go to Clark's Woods," one of the boys said. "Maybe we can find that owl again."

"Not me," the other said. "It was scary the way he just sat there looking at us."

Jacob looked out the window while he listened to the talk behind him. There were old farmhouses, painted white with green shutters. Many of the trees in the woods had lost their leaves in the winds of autumn.

The road was still new to him, not at all like the city

streets where he had spent most of his life. But he liked his new home. He loved the woods and the wild creatures he saw there.

"That old owl kept so still," one of the boys behind him said.

"Yeah, those big eyes just kept staring at us," the other boy said.

Jacob wished that he could ask some questions about the owl. He had never seen a live owl. What an adventure for those boys, he thought, to come suddenly upon this large wild bird in the deep woods!

How big was the owl? Was it sitting in a tree when the boys saw it? Jacob had already explored Clark's Woods. Was the owl at the edge of the woods?

But Jacob did not ask any questions. He had come to the school that fall. He did not make friends very easily. In fact, he had no friends at his new school.

"I would hate to meet that owl on a dark night," one of the boys said.

Jacob listened so hard that he was home before he knew it. The bus came to a stop in front of his house. When he got off the bus, no one said goodbye, or even paid any attention to him.

He shut the heavy door of the old farmhouse behind him. His mother had rented the house from a friend when she and Jacob moved to this town in northern New England. They had been there for only three months, and it was new and strange to him.

"How was school today?" his mother called from

the living room. She was home from work early today.

"Okay," Jacob called back. He did not say anything about what was on his mind.

But the owl was very much on his mind. He went upstairs to his small bedroom, where the ceiling sloped down toward a small window. He looked out the window and saw the tops of the trees in Clark's Woods.

He stood at the window, holding the curtain to one side. In his mind he saw a dark, wide-eyed owl, sitting in a tree in the gloom of the woods.

A picture of the owl seemed to stay with him all night. Once or twice he woke up. Had he heard the hooting of an owl? He could not be sure. But each time he closed his eyes again there was a picture of the owl, bright in his mind.

Discovery

Jacob went to the woods on Saturday morning.

He was a thin boy, with large, dark eyes that seemed to glow in his pale face. But now, dressed warmly against the cold wind of late October, he looked almost husky. He wore a heavy jacket and gloves.

Clark's Woods were the only part of his new home town that seemed familiar to him. They reminded him of the woods around the boys' camp where he had spent last summer. He had made no friends there. He had liked to explore the woods by himself.

He had found secret places in the woods at camp. One of them had been a little pool, surrounded by moss-covered rocks. Once he had caught a frog by the pool. Another time he had caught a small snake.

The director of the camp had never let him keep the animals he captured. Jacob had taken the animals back to the pool and set them free. No one else at camp had ever found his secret place.

Clark's Woods, near his new home, stood between two farmhouses along the main road from town. Jacob walked in among the trees. It was darker than he thought it would be in the woods. The birch trees along the road had lost most of their leaves.

But beyond the birches there were many spruce trees. The spruces kept their dark green needles all year long. It was hard to see through their thick growth.

Jacob walked along a path through the trees. Is the owl still in the woods? The boys on the school bus had said it sat very quietly. Could he find the owl in the dark spruces?

Jacob heard a sound above him. He looked up and saw a red squirrel, standing on a branch high above him.

"*Chick-chick-chick!*" the squirrel seemed to say. It was scolding him.

Jacob walked on. He felt that the woods were alive. Chickadees—tiny birds with black caps—flew through the trees. The squirrel still scolded from its branch. The owl must be here too, among all this life.

Jacob had never seen a live owl. Yet the boys' story made the owl seem very real. The bird seemed to be close to him all week.

"Jay! Jay! Jay!" the blue jays seemed to shout.

The long-tailed birds were very excited. They were hopping around a chunky, dark form in a tree near the path. They were scolding it, just as the squirrel had scolded Jacob.

He walked toward the tree. When he came near, the blue jays flew away. At that instant Jacob found himself looking into the wide, dark eyes of the owl.

The boy and the owl stared at each other for a long time. Jacob was not sure how long he stood there. Sometimes the owl blinked, but it never took its eyes off the boy. It sat on the branch with its dark brown feathers fluffed up in an odd way.

Jacob took a step toward the owl. He wanted more than anything in the world to touch this large, fluffy, brown bird. He stretched his arm toward the bird, and was startled when it suddenly flapped its wings and flew out of the tree.

Jacob was frightened. But the owl did not threaten him. It flew in a crooked way across the path toward another tree.

The owl never reached the tree. It turned partly on its side in the air and crashed into the leaves on the ground. Its wings were still spread wide. It struggled to close them and stand on its feet. Then the owl turned to face Jacob, clacking its short curved beak.

Giving Owl a Home

The owl stood on newspapers that covered a small table in a corner of the kitchen. It never took its eyes off the boy and the woman.

"Oh, yes," Jacob's mother said. "It is a beautiful bird. Its eyes are so big and such a deep rich brown—like some wonderful jewels."

"Then I can keep the owl!" Jacob said with excitement.

His mother was silent. She ran her hand through her light hair and went on looking at the owl.

"No, Jacob," she said, turning now to look at the boy. "It is beautiful, but we can't keep it here."

"I had pets in the city," Jacob said, the excitement still in his voice. "A canary, remember? And the gerbil. I took care of them all right."

"But that was different, Jacob," his mother said. "You took care of them just as you said you would. But they were small animals that were raised as pets. This is a wild creature. You can't keep it in a house."

Jacob was surprised and hurt. He and his mother had always been close. They were together more than ever since his father left home to live in California. Jacob did not understand why his mother and father had decided not to live together. He only knew that all three of them felt sadness at being apart.

He and his mother seldom talked about their life with his father in the city. They were both very busy since

coming to live in the old farmhouse. Each day Jacob took the bus to school in the nearby town. His mother drove her small car to the local hospital, where she worked in a laboratory.

"I can fix up a home for the owl in the shed," Jacob insisted. "I can take care of it. There's something wrong with its wing. If we turn it loose, it will die."

His mother was silent again. She walked slowly to the table and stretched her hand toward the owl. The owl shuffled backward and clacked its beak together sharply. Its right wing did not close completely.

The woman stroked the owl lightly on its head. The bird seemed to grow calm under her touch. She ran her fingers over the right wing.

"I think the wing was hurt some time ago," she said to Jacob. "If it was broken, it is partly healed now. But it is still crooked and the owl can't fly straight anymore. It must have trouble catching mice to eat."

"So we have to feed it," Jacob said.

"Yes, it looks hungry," his mother said. "It looks sick, with its feathers all fluffed up like that. We'll feed it, and then we will find some place else for it to live."

Jacob pretended not to hear the last part of what his mother said. He was already on his way to the woodshed that was connected to the house.

"I'll make a place for Owl in the shed," he said, the excitement coming back into his voice. "Owl—that's what he is, so that's what I'll call him."

The First Test

"Owl won't eat."

Jacob was close to tears. He looked from his mother to the dish that held the ground meat. Owl simply looked at Jacob, and paid no attention to the food.

Owl stood on a log that Jacob had set under the window. The only light in the shed came in through the dusty windowpanes. The branch of an old tree brushed the outside wall of the shed.

Long ago, the shed had been a place where the owners of the house stored wood for the cookstove. Now there was just a rickety table and some broken chairs. They seemed to be held together only by the cobwebs that covered them.

The late afternoon sun streamed in on Owl, shining on him like a spotlight. The rest of the shed lay in shadows and musty smells.

"Eat. Please."

"Break up some of the ground meat and hold it to Owl's beak," Jacob's mother said. "I have to go and start dinner."

Jacob was left alone with Owl. On his right hand the boy wore a long leather glove that his mother had found for him in a closet. It came up over his wrist and lower arm. Owl's beak looked harmless enough, but his talons—or claws—were long and sharp.

Jacob lifted a few shreds of beef toward Owl's beak. The bird drew back his head and clapped the upper and lower parts of his beak together:

"*Clack! Clack! Clack!*"

Jacob pulled back his hand quickly. The sharp sounds were a warning, he thought.

"If you don't eat, you'll starve," he pleaded with Owl.

Owl simply held the boy in his direct stare. The great dark eyes remained motionless in the broad, flat face. The yellow beak stayed firmly closed. The brown feathers, tipped with white, turned golden in the fading sun.

"I won't hurt you," Jacob said softly.

He held the beef in his gloved hand, almost touching Owl's beak. Owl still paid no attention.

Jacob put the beef back in the dish and returned Owl's stare. The bird looked as if he were just a huge head, and nothing more. The face, with its great staring eyes, lay in a circle of fluff.

Jacob took off the glove and stretched his fingers toward the top of Owl's head. Owl stiffened, and clacked his beak. But the boy laid his fingers lightly on the puffy head. The feathers felt unbelievably soft. He stroked them gently.

Owl remained still. He blinked, showing the feathery tips of his eyelids. Beneath the feathery lids were inner lids that slid up over part of the eyes like a purple film and then disappeared.

Jacob went on stroking Owl's head. He wondered if there was a skull of real bone beneath that soft mass of feathers. But he was afraid to push all the way down to find out.

He took some beef from the dish again and held it

to Owl's beak. Owl paid no attention. Then, growing bolder, Jacob stretched his bare hand to the beak and rubbed it gently with the beef. Owl still paid no attention, but he did not move his head away.

The boy went on gently rubbing the beef against the sharply curved beak. It was almost dusk before Owl stirred. Jacob could barely see any movement at first. He just felt the beak move slowly. He could not be sure that it really opened.

Suddenly, Jacob realized that the little ball of ground beef was gone from his hand. He had never felt such excitement. He reached into the dish and held up more beef to the beak. This time there was no doubt about it. Owl opened his beak and swallowed the meat.

In a little while the dish was empty. Owl fluffed up his feathers. He stood taller on the log, spread his wings wide, and half-flew, half-hopped, to the back of a chair against the wall. He perched there in the dim light, smoothing his breast feathers with gentle strokes of his beak.

Jacob left the shed quietly, but he was running by the time he reached the kitchen.

"Mom, he ate!"

His mother smiled, but did not say anything.

That evening Jacob ate his own dinner thoughtfully. He had found a friend. He did not know how long this friendship would last.

A Letter

Dear Dad,

I was glad to get a letter from you. It sounds like California is just great.

Thanks for sending me the new jacket. It got very cold here at Christmas. It snowed twice.

As a rule, Jacob did not like to write letters. But so many exciting things had happened to him that he wanted to share them with somebody.

His father had written to him from his new home in California. He had told Jacob about his job as a telephone repairman. Jacob had some interesting things to tell his father, too.

Owl looks better. His wing still looks funny. But mother brings home dead mice from the science lab. Owl eats 2 or 3 mice every day.

Jacob wrote the letter at the little table in his room where he did his homework. On his wall there were color pictures that he had clipped from magazines. There were pictures of a tiger and an eagle and a family of chimps.

His room was over the shed where Owl had lived since he found him almost three months before. He could hear Owl moving around. Sometimes Owl flew against the window and scratched it. Sometimes Owl hopped from the back of a chair to the floor with a loud thump.

I wear heavy gloves when I pick up Owl. He sits on my

"Owl is okay this morning," he said, breaking the silence. "I calmed him down."

"Yes, Jacob, I know you did," his mother said, reaching across the table to touch his hand. "You handled Owl beautifully."

Then she became silent again. The silence made Jacob uneasy. Several times in recent weeks his mother had said that it made her sad to see Owl cooped up in the shed. Maybe if she had her own owl, Jacob said to himself, she would not be sad.

The accident last night made Jacob even more uneasy. He had found Owl crouched on the floor, badly frightened.

The wind outside was blowing hard. It had blown a branch against the window of the shed. Owl, probably startled by the noise, had tried to fly out of the shed. The bird had beaten its wings against the walls in a panic. Finally it had fallen to the floor, exhausted.

Jacob's mother said little as they cleared away the breakfast dishes. He knew that something was bothering her. When she asked him to help her with the shopping, he quickly agreed to go with her.

They finished shopping and put the bundles in the car. But then Jacob's mother did not turn toward home. Instead, she drove on toward another town.

"Where are we going?" Jacob asked.

"We're going to a place that I think both of us will be interested to see," his mother said. "I heard about it from some friends at the hospital. It's a special kind of bird sanctuary."

She drove off the main road and up a winding lane. The lane was lined with tall trees. At the end of the lane stood a house, with some smaller buildings behind it.

"This is a sanctuary, where wild birds are protected," Jacob's mother said as she drove up in front of the house. "The man who runs the sanctuary also cares for birds that have been injured."

They walked along a gravel path past the house. Jacob realized that the smaller buildings were really large cages covered with wire. He stopped short at the first cage. Staring at him from behind the wire were four owls. Each of them looked exactly like Owl.

Jacob was frightened, and then angry. He had been tricked. This was what his mother wanted to do with Owl—take him away and put him in this big cage with all the other owls.

"I'm not going to give up Owl," he said in a low voice.

At that moment a door opened and a man walked out of the house. He wore a dark jacket and carried a small knife in one hand. The winter sun glinted on his eyeglasses. Jacob watched him with distrust.

But when the man spoke, he did so in a friendly voice.

"So this is the young fellow you told me about on the phone," he said, looking at Jacob. "I hear you found a barred owl. Your mother says you have done a wonderful job nursing it back to health."

"It still can't fly," was all that Jacob said in reply.

"Don't be alarmed by this knife," the man said, "I've been cutting up chicken parts to feed an injured hawk."

Jacob remained uneasy. He listened carefully, however, as his mother and the man talked about the birds in the cages.

He learned that the man's name was Mr. Redmond. People from all the nearby towns brought injured wild birds to him. Some of these birds had been hit by cars. Others had run into telephone wires or had been shot.

"It looks as if many people bring birds here," Jacob's mother said.

"It takes a great deal of time to care for any wild creature," Mr. Redmond said. "Many people try it for a while, but then they get busy with other things, and the bird is the one that suffers."

Jacob could no longer stay silent.

"I would never get tired of taking care of Owl," he said excitedly. "Owl is my best friend."

"Well, I believe you would do everything you could for Owl," Mr. Redmond said seriously. "Naturally, people who find an injured bird want to help it. But you cannot keep a wild bird for a long time."

Jacob watched the man's face intently.

"You must bring it to a government agency or to a sanctuary that has a license to care for birds if they are sick or injured," Mr. Redmond went on. "This is how the government protects owls and most other kinds of wild birds from being misused or needlessly caged."

Jacob could hardly believe what he had just heard. He turned to his mother anxiously. She took his hand.

"Oh, we had no idea that birds were protected this way," she said to Mr. Redmond.

Jacob did not hear any more of the conversation. He was too upset by what he had already heard. He was only thankful that his mother did not say anything to him on the drive home.

A Special Friend

Jacob worked very hard to give Owl a good home. He did not tell anyone in school about his special friend. But he could hardly wait to return home in the afternoons and work in the shed.

He tried not to think about what Mr. Redmond had told him. He swept the floor, dusted the broken chairs, and spread clean newspapers and paper towels under the logs where Owl liked to perch. He washed the window and set a perching log on a table so that Owl could see outside.

He changed the water in the big dish where Owl drank and bathed. He fed Owl the mice that his mother brought home from the lab. He even searched the roads near home to bring back to Owl the small animals that had been killed by cars.

Jacob made good use of what he read about owls. He read that barred owls often nest in the hollows of trees. So he put a wooden box in the shed where Owl could sleep. He read that owls like to lean against tree trunks. So he put a perching log against the wall where Owl could lean against it.

Owl had no fear of Jacob. When the boy pulled on the heavy glove, Owl hopped up onto his wrist. He perched there quietly while Jacob talked to him in a soft voice or stroked the feathers on his round, puffy head.

Every time his mother mentioned the sanctuary, Jacob fell silent or left the room. She did not order him to give up Owl. She seemed to know how deeply he felt about his special friend. But he lived with the fear that Owl would be taken from him.

"Come up here, Owl," he coaxed, extending his hand.

Owl looked up at the boy from the perch. The talons released their grip on the log, the wings opened part way, and the owl sprang onto Jacob's wrist. He carried the bird out into the bright sunlight.

The small woodland birds set up an excited chatter at the sight of the big brown owl. Some of them scolded from the tree tops. Others flew off into the woods.

Jacob tried to imagine Owl as a fierce wild creature. He knew from his books that barred owls see well in daylight, but hunt mostly at dusk and dawn.

He wondered if Owl, so still now on his wrist, ever dreamed of the wild. Ever dreamed of perching in the forest at twilight, listening for the slightest sound in the leaf piles below, and flying true as an arrow to strike some furry animal on the ground.

For the hundredth time, Jacob's free hand touched the long talons that gripped his gloved wrist. They were as cold and shiny as steel. They were the weapons of a hunter. Jacob had seen them seize a dead mouse. It was easy to imagine how swiftly those talons would kill an animal in the forest.

With his fingers he lifted the feathers on one side of Owl's head. Beneath them was the bird's ear. It was bordered by other small feathers that the owl spread to catch faint sounds in the forest. Barred owls, the books said, caught animals that they could not see in the dark.

It was hard to believe. Yet what he had read about an owl's marvelous hearing gave Jacob an idea.

That evening, when it was dark, Jacob took one of the dead mice his mother had brought home from the lab. He tied a thread tightly to its tail. Then he slipped into the shed.

He could not see Owl in the pitch-dark. He gently laid the mouse on the floor across the shed from Owl's perch. Taking the thread with him, he left the shed and closed the door.

Jacob got down on his hands and knees. He pulled the thread to draw the dead mouse across the floor toward the door. Suddenly, there was a thud. The thread was almost pulled from his hand. Owl had the mouse tightly in his talons.

Jacob grew worried. If Owl swallowed the mouse, he would swallow the long piece of thread, too. Jacob pulled on the thread with all his might. Owl would not let go.

The thread snapped. With a sigh of relief, Jacob found that most of the thread slid easily under the door. Owl would swallow only the little knot left on the tail.

Jacob was proud of his friend. Owl's crippled wing might prevent him from flying free, but he still kept many of the skills and instincts of the night hunter—the sharp hearing, the strong talons.

"You might not have school tomorrow, Jacob," his mother called as he came in from the shed. "They said on television that a big storm is coming."

The Storm

A bitter wind swept out of the morning sky. The tops of the trees snapped like whips.

The school bus stopped in front of Jacob's house as usual and he was disappointed that he would not be able to spend the day with Owl. The wind blew hard all morning. After lunch the icy snow began to fall. Winter had not given up its hold on the land.

School was dismissed in early afternoon. Jacob felt happy as he climbed aboard the bus because he would have more time to spend with Owl. Branches and twigs cluttered the road, blown from the trees by the swirling wind. The snow stuck to the windows of the bus.

Jacob let himself into the house and rushed to the shed. He reached for the latch on the door. But he knew at once that something was wrong.

The wind whistled through cracks in the door. He threw open the door and a blast of wet snow struck him in the face.

"Owl! Owl!" he cried.

Owl was not in the shed. A heavy branch was still beating against the shattered window.

Jacob ran out into the wind and snow. In a protected place, between the shed and the tree, he thought he could make out faint tracks—the print of a foot with long talons, the marks left by a wing beating frantically on the snow.

He tried to make out other tracks. But, in the open

ground beyond the tree, the wind had swept the snow clean of any marks.

Jacob looked toward the distant woods. There—a dark form in that tree! He broke into a run, breathlessly fighting the snow that the wind hurled into his face. He tripped and fell. He struggled back to his feet and raced on.

When he reached the tree, he held on to the trunk with both hands and looked up. He saw the dark form of rotting leaves, perhaps piled into a fork in the branches by a squirrel many months before. It was not Owl at all.

The snow swirled harder than ever from the sky. Jacob could hardly see. There was nothing around him but a white, windy world. Fear came over him. He turned and ran back toward the house.

"My fault! My fault!" he sobbed over and over. If only he had cut that loose branch by the shed's window.

The Dream

Jacob slept badly that night. At last he fell into a troubled sleep and had a dream.

There was an owl in a tree deep in the woods. The owl was frightened. Jacob felt the fear intensely.

He looked down to find himself covered by feathers.

They were a rich brown, broadly tipped with white. They were fringed with soft tufts so that when he flapped his wings they made no sound. They were the wings of a night hunter who could fly silently through the forest.

A boy was following him. There was also a man, with white hair, who wore eyeglasses that glinted in the sun. Jacob flew deeper into the forest.

He was alone and frightened. He was growing hungry. He saw a mouse in the leaves on the forest floor. There was another mouse, and another. Mice were all around him.

Jacob's muscles grew tense as he prepared to strike. He lifted a foot tipped with black steely talons.

But something had happened to them. They were not like steel anymore. They were as limp as worms. The mice scurried through the leaves.

Jacob ran his curved beak through his feathers, smoothing them into place. But they would not stay in place. They snapped up and stuck out in all directions.

He nibbled at the feathers. They came out in bunches in his bill.

He looked up and saw a friend. His heart beat with excitement. A boy was rushing toward him through the forest.

Jacob lifted his wings. He flapped them once, twice, and sprang into the air. As he began to fly, the rest of his feathers were torn out by the bitter wind.

He felt himself falling. Falling down toward the forest floor, where the mice went on feeding in the leaves.

Search

The weeks passed. Owl did not return from the woods.

The wet snow disappeared in March. Pools of water lay in the soggy earth. Jacob saw the buds swell and grow red on the trees.

Jacob looked for Owl everywhere. His eyes were never still.

He imagined he saw Owl, wings spread wide, in the clouds that hung low over the forest.

He saw Owl in the shape of a distant stump, or the burst of new leaves in a woodland tree.

He thought he saw Owl's dark feathers reflected in pools and ponds.

Jacob sat for hours by the window in his room, looking for a sign. He stared out the window of the school bus, not hearing the chatter of the boys and girls around him.

At first his sadness was mixed with pride, and almost a sense of relief. Owl had chosen freedom. He was a fierce hunter again, flashing down from his perch in the twilight to strike some careless woodland creature.

But the sense of relief lasted only a short time. With a sinking feeling, Jacob realized that Owl was not a skillful hunter anymore. He had been gone for nearly a month.

Only the strongest animals can live in the wild. Owl might find a sick or helpless creature once in a while. But it took two strong wings for an owl to be a great hunter.

Jacob's mother knew how bad he felt. She took him

to the movies and she made his favorite desserts. She tried to get him to join the young people's club at their church.

"You could go with Nelson, the boy down the road," she said.

But Jacob was not interested in movies. He was never hungry, even for blueberry pie with vanilla ice cream. He did not feel like making friends.

Something had gone out of Jacob's life. He could not imagine anything that would take its place.

A Tap at the Window

"You really ought to go on this camping trip," Jacob's mother said to him. "The young people's club at the church has gone to a lot of trouble, and you'll see a new part of the state."

"I guess I won't go," he said.

"Nelson's mother told me that he is going, and I know he would like to be your friend," his mother went on.

"I don't have any friends," Jacob said. He knew that his words sounded grumpy, so he added, "I just guess I won't go."

"That's a shame. I even arranged to borrow a down sleeping bag for you from the club in case it got cold during the night."

Jacob felt a little ashamed of himself. His mother was doing all she could to get him interested in new activities. But he simply did not feel like going anywhere.

In the morning it was very cold. The temperature had dropped during the night and a film of frost coated the window panes. He was glad to be snug in his own bed, and not camping somewhere in the mountains.

He lay in bed, half-asleep. He heard a sound from the shed below. There was a thump, and a sound like scratching.

The noise was painful for him to hear. It must be that darn old branch, scraping up against the shed in the wind. The branch he should have cut.

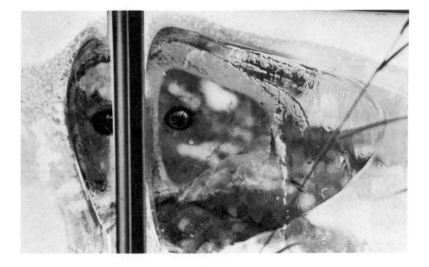

He lay back in his warm bed. He could see the tops of trees, straight and still, through the frosty glass. Nice and still. The scratching sound came from the shed again.

Jacob sat up with a start. Nice and still. The treetops were not swaying in the wind. Then why was the wind blowing a branch against the shed?

He put on his bathrobe and went downstairs. He looked inside the shed. The window was frosted over, and behind it was a dark form. He rushed to the window and peered out.

"Owl!"

Trembling with the cold and excitement, Jacob opened the window. Owl stood on the ledge—looking pretty awful, but still Owl. Jacob stepped back, and the bird flapped into the shed and landed on his old perching log.

Owl stared at Jacob through eyes half-shut. His feathers were ruffled, and several of them were broken. He sat hunched up, wings slightly open, as if too tired and hungry to look the part of a fierce hunter. But Owl was alive.

Jacob just stared at him for a long time. Then he closed the window and began to talk through his chattering teeth.

"Owl, where have you been? What happened? Oh, you didn't find enough to eat."

The long leather glove still lay on the rickety table where Jacob had last put it down. He pulled it on and lifted Owl onto his wrist.

"We don't have any mice for you," he said to his special friend. "We thought you were dead. So it's back to hamburger for today."

And Jacob buried his face in the soft brown feathers.

Mr. Redmond

The four barred owls stared sleepily at Jacob through the wire that covered their large cage. They were the first birds Jacob saw when he got out of his mother's car at the sanctuary. The sight of those four owls made him unhappy.

Jacob did not want to make this second visit to the sanctuary. His mother had asked him to come with her. He did not want to hurt her feelings by saying no.

Mr. Redmond came out of his house to meet them. His eyes were friendly behind the glasses.

"I'm glad you got your owl back, Jacob," he said. "How is it doing?"

"Okay," Jacob said.

He did not feel like talking. He still thought of Mr. Redmond as someone who wanted to come between him and Owl. If I am not careful, he thought, Mr. Redmond will take Owl away from me and stick him in that cage with all the other owls.

On second thought, Jacob decided to let Mr. Redmond know that he was eleven years old and caring for Owl was not a problem for him.

"I'm feeding Owl lots of mice," Jacob said proudly. "Yesterday I brought him a squirrel that got run over by a car."

Then he walked over to the cage to look at the barred owls. He did not want Mr. Redmond to ask him questions about how Owl was lost. But Mr. Redmond now seemed to be talking only to Jacob's mother.

"Some people believe it's best not to try to help wild animals that are sick or injured," Mr. Redmond said. "They say we should leave them to nature. But most of the birds that are brought here have been injured because of something we human beings have made—cars, guns, electric wires. I think it's only fair, then, that we try to help."

Jacob's mother looked at the boy to see if he was listening. Then she turned back to Mr. Redmond.

"Can you help all the birds and animals that people bring here?" she asked.

"Some of them are too badly injured to be helped," the man said. "They die very quickly. But we fix up more than half of them so that they can live a fairly normal life."

Jacob looked closely at the owls in the big cage. They perched quietly on thick branches that Mr. Redmond had brought there for them. One owl nibbled softly at the neck feathers of the owl next to it.

"Do you know which owl is which?" Jacob asked Mr. Redmond.

The man laughed. "Yes," he said. "We keep records on all of them, and we can tell one from another."

Jacob was silent for a few moments. He did not like to admit it, but all of the owls in the cage looked well cared for and content.

"What happens if you get sick? Who takes care of all of these birds?"

"Jacob, any time you want to come and help me, you will be welcome," Mr. Redmond said. "There's lots of work to be done here."

Jacob was thoughtful on the way home. No one had mentioned Owl again at the sanctuary, but he did not quite trust Mr. Redmond. He would have to be careful.

An Invitation

"Jacob, here is a letter from your father."

Jacob took the letter from his mother. He opened it eagerly and read his father's invitation:

Dear Jacob,

I hope you will be able to come and live with me for a while in California when school is out. Your mother thinks it is a good idea, and I hope you do, too.

The mountains are beautiful. There are lots of birds and other animals. I know a swift-running stream where we can go fishing together.

The letter made Jacob very happy. It made him feel very close to his father. He thought about the letter for a long time.

"I'm not going to California," he told his mother at last.

"But, Jacob, your father wants to see you. You will have a wonderful time with him. And afterward, you will have so many adventures to tell me about."

"I'm not going," Jacob said.

"Don't you want to go?" his mother asked.

"Yes. But—I can't go!"

Jacob turned and rushed into the shed. He tried to hold back his tears when his mother followed him through the door. He ran his fingers through the soft feathers on Owl's head.

"Don't come in here," he said to his mother in a hard voice.

His mother was close to tears, too.

"You know you have to make up your mind about Owl soon," she said. "You cared for Owl when he needed help. But he is a wild bird, and he needs more freedom and special care than we can give him. He needs to be with other birds of his kind."

"I can take care of Owl," Jacob said. "I know I can take care of him."

"We are away from the house all day," his mother went on. "Owl might get away again, and you know that he just can't take care of himself properly in the woods."

The boy said nothing. He stroked Owl's head. The owl blinked his large dark eyes.

"Jacob, your father loves you very much," his mother said. "He wants you to come and live with him for a while. You belong to him as much as to me."

Jacob walked over to his mother and threw his arms around her. He still did not say anything.

"Why don't you go to the sanctuary tomorrow?" she said softly. "I'm sure that Mr. Redmond can use some help."

A New Friend

It was a very busy Saturday morning in spring for Jacob. He brought fresh water to the barred owls in their cage at the sanctuary. He put fruit and seed in a large cage where songbirds—robins, sparrows, and catbirds—flitted from perch to perch. He arranged fresh, leafy branches in the cage to make it more like the songbirds' woodland home.

He looked forward now each week to working at the

sanctuary. He knew the names of all the birds and what injuries kept them there. The tiny saw-whet owl with the bright brown and yellow eyes had only one wing. The broad-winged hawk had been shot.

"The robin that's pecking at the apple will be able to leave the cage soon," Mr. Redmond said. "As soon as we get a good stretch of weather, I'll set it free."

Mr. Redmond did his best to care for every wild creature that was brought to him. He treated their wounds. He made good homes for them. But what gave him the greatest satisfaction was to watch a bird recover so that he could give it back its freedom.

Someone had brought a barred owl to the sanctuary the night before. The bird had been hit by a car. Mr. Redmond put a splint on its broken wing. But the owl refused to eat.

"I could try to open its beak and push in some food," Mr. Redmond told Jacob. "But I would rather have the owl really want to eat by itself. Sometimes you can play tricks on a bird."

Jacob remembered how much trouble he had gone through getting Owl to eat. He watched as Mr. Redmond began to play a trick on the owl.

The older man took a dead mouse and carefully twisted its head and feet into life-like positions. Then he put it on the floor of the owl's cage. He partly covered the mouse with some leaves. The mouse looked as if it were crouched in the leaves, ready to run away.

At first the owl paid no attention to what the man was putting on the floor of its cage. It was more interested in the man himself. But when the man and the boy stepped back from the cage, the owl saw the mouse. It stared hard at the tiny animal in the leaves.

Mr. Redmond made a sound like a squeaking mouse. The owl stared even harder at the mouse.

"The owl knows the sound I made isn't coming from the mouse," Mr. Redmond whispered. "But I am hoping that the sound will get the owl thinking about the taste of mice. It might even think that the mouse is going to escape."

Jacob held his breath. The owl remained still only a moment longer. When Mr. Redmond squeaked again, the owl sprang into action.

The bird dropped from the perch, talons spread. It landed squarely on the mouse and clutched it firmly. Then the owl hopped back to its perch and swallowed the mouse.

"That was a great sound you made," Jacob said to Mr. Redmond. "How did you do it?"

The man showed Jacob how to hold his mouth and tongue. Jacob tried, and found himself squeaking like a mouse. He and Mr. Redmond burst out laughing.

"Owls are like people in some ways," Mr. Redmond said. "They want to feel they can be on their own just like we do. If an owl is able to do something it is supposed to do in the wild—like catch a mouse—it is bound to feel better."

Jacob watched the owl in the big cage.

"Do you think this owl will get better?" he asked.

Mr. Redmond nodded. "I think it will," he said. "That is not a bad break in its wing. I think that in a few weeks we can turn the bird loose, as good as new."

"But Owl can never be turned loose," Jacob said.

"No, because from what you tell me, Owl can't really fly anymore," the man said. "But there are birds like Owl right here at the sanctuary that can never leave. They are valuable, too. People come from all over to look at them and begin to learn what marvelous creatures birds are. They begin to think more about liking and protecting wild birds."

Jacob was more thoughtful than usual as he went back to his chores around the big cages. At the end of the day he stopped at the house to say good-bye to Mr. Redmond.

"I won't be able to help you for a while," he told him. "I'm going to California."

Mr. Redmond smiled at him. He did not say that Jacob's mother had already told him about his difficult decision.

"I thought you were going to tell me that, Jacob," he said.

Going On

Jacob stopped at the sanctuary on his way to the airport. His mother remained in the car while he ran up the path to the house. His spirits were high.

"You're just in time," Mr. Redmond called to him.

The man stood on the lawn, holding one of the barred owls from the cage. The sunlight on Mr. Redmond's glasses seemed to reflect the happy twinkle in his eyes.

"I'm going to set this bird loose," he said. "Its wing is healed. It is ready to go back home. I'll bet it heads straight for the river, and then off into the woods on the other side."

Mr. Redmond held the owl in both hands. He turned in the direction of the river, and tossed the bird lightly

into the air. It flapped aimlessly for a moment, then seemed to realize it was free, and flew away toward the river.

"I think that's the most beautiful sight in the world," Mr. Redmond said, the smile still on his face. "It always gives me a thrill to be able to send a bird back to its life in the wild."

A soft expression of wonder came over Jacob's face. "Oh!" was all that he could say as he watched the bird fly on slowly beating wings across the nearby river.

"Well, you are going on a flight of your own, young man," Mr. Redmond said to him.

Jacob nodded. His eyes were still shining.

"I have my ticket in my pocket," he said. "Mother gave me twenty dollars for spending money. And Nelson, my new friend at school, loaned me a book about African animals to read on the plane."

He walked to the large cage where four barred owls sat on perches. One barred owl had just flown to freedom. But Owl sat on a perch, taking its place.

When Jacob reached the cage, Owl hopped to the wire. Jacob stroked the feathers on his throat through the wire. Owl playfully nibbled at the boy's fingers.

"He looks good," Jacob said to Mr. Redmond. "Better than ever."

It was his way of saying "thank you" to the older man.

"I've been giving Owl some vitamins with his mice," Mr. Redmond said. "He's living a good life here, these last two weeks. Owls live a long time, and he is still young. I'll bet that even when you are grown up, you will come back from college and visit Owl here."

"I wish he could fly back to the woods," Jacob said.

"Owls learn how to make the best of things, just like we do," Mr. Redmond said. "Owl was lucky that he had you for a friend when he needed one."

Jacob looked down as Owl nibbled his finger again.

"I was lucky, too." he said.